P9-BIQ-642

Disney's
Winnie the Pooh's Christmas

Disney's
Winnie the Pooh's Christmas

Written *by* Bruce Talkington

Illustrated *by* Alvin S. White Studio

Pencils by Sparky Moore

Backgrounds by Gene Ware

DISNEY
PRESS

NEW YORK

Copyright © 1991 by Disney Press.
All rights reserved. No part of this book may be used or reproduced
in any manner whatsoever without written permission from the publisher.
Printed in the United States of America.
For information address Disney Press, 114 Fifth Avenue, New York, New York 10011.
Based on the Pooh stories by A. A. Milne (copyright The Pooh Properties Trust).

FIRST PAPERBACK EDITION
5 7 9 10 8 6

Library of Congress Catalog Card Number: 91-71353

ISBN: 0-7868-4010-2

Disney's

Winnie the Pooh's Christmas

I t was the night before Christmas, and Winnie the Pooh's nose was pressed flat against a windowpane. He was gazing out at the snow hushing the Hundred-Acre Wood, gathering cozily like bedclothes around the house where he lived.

"I'm very glad to see you," Pooh chuckled to the plump snowflakes drifting past. "You're just in time for Christmas, which, if you must be in time for something, is something very nice to be in time for!"

Pooh turned to take a look at his house full of decorations. "Let me see, a tree, some candles..." He scratched his head and sighed. "There seems to be something... missing!"

All at once Pooh heard a rattle of very small knocks at his front door. "Perhaps," Pooh smiled to himself, "that is whatever it is that's missing!"

Pooh opened the door to find a very small snowman with a pair of very Piglet-looking ears.

"Oh!" remarked Pooh, who was a very surprised bear. Then he added, "Hello!" to be polite, because one should always be polite, even to surprises.

"H-h-hello, P-Pooh B-Bear," the snowman answered in a very Piglet-sounding voice. "M-Merry Christmas!"

Pooh wondered whether it was more polite to invite the snowman in where it was warm or let him stay outside where snowmen are usually more comfortable. The snowman finally gave Pooh a very small hint. "May I come in?" it asked.

"Please do," said Pooh.

The snowman hurried inside and stood before the fireplace. "The only thing I don't like about Christmas," said the snowman, "and it's a very small thing, is that my ears get so very cold."

"I can imagine," replied Pooh, who could not imagine a snowman's ears being anything but cold.

The snowman stood shivering in front of the fire and, with every tremble and quiver, began to look less and less like a snowman and more and more like Piglet!

"Why, hello, Piglet!" blurted Pooh, delighted to see his very small, very best friend standing in a puddle of water on the hearth where a snowman had stood just moments before. "If I had known it was you, I would have invited you in!"

Piglet smiled up at his friend. "Oh, Pooh! You *did* invite me in! You knew it was me all along."

"Well, of course I did, Piglet," responded Pooh, scratching his head. "I just didn't know I knew until this particular moment."

"My!" breathed Piglet in wonder as he gazed up at Pooh's Christmas tree, glimmering golden in the candlelight. Glowing candles hung from its branches, each nestled in its own honeypot. "I've never seen so many candles on one tree."

"Well," explained Pooh, "there seemed to be a great many empty honeypots to use for candleholders. And there was a great deal of extra room on the tree because the popcorn didn't seem to get strung."

"Would you like me to help you string the popcorn, Pooh?" Piglet asked.

"Why, yes, Piglet. I'd like that very much," answered Pooh. "That is, if there were any popcorn left to string,

which there isn't."

"Oh dear," said Piglet. He looked around nervously, leaned close to Pooh, and whispered, "What happened to it all?"

"I ate it," Pooh whispered back. "I was tasting it to make sure it was properly popped, and by the time I was sure," Pooh shrugged and sighed, "it was all gone. I do, however, still have the string."

"That's all right, Pooh!" Piglet laughed. "We can use the string to wrap your gifts!"

"But, Piglet," chuckled Pooh, "the gifts won't be here until tomorrow morning. And then I *unwrap* them." Pooh leaned close and whispered confidentially into Piglet's ear. "That's the way it's done, you know." There may have been a few things about Christmas on which Pooh was a little hazy, but opening presents wasn't one of them.

"No, Pooh, I mean I'll help you wrap the presents you're going to *give*!"

Pooh's smile disappeared. "Oh!" he said quietly. "*Those* gifts." Then even more quietly, he added, "Oh bother!"

"What's the matter, Pooh?" Piglet asked.

Pooh sighed tremendously. "I think I just remembered what I forgot," he said. "It's presents."

"No presents?" Piglet looked up at Pooh sadly. "Not

even a very small one?"

Pooh shook his head. "I'm sorry, Piglet."

Piglet smiled bravely. "It's all right, Pooh. I always get a bit too excited opening presents. And it's the thought that counts, you know," he sniffed. "I think I'll take my very cold ears and go home."

Pooh saw his friend to the door and watched him walk sadly down the path as the snowflakes began turning him into a very small snowman once again.

"Oh my," Pooh said to himself as he wound his muffler around his neck and stepped out into the snow. "If it's the thought that counts at Christmas, I think I'd better ask Christopher Robin what *he* thinks about thoughts and presents and Christmas and everything."

It was a long, chilly tramp through the swirling night. The snowflakes tickled Pooh's nose and crept down the back of his neck to get warm. He was very glad when he arrived at Christopher Robin's house, and he knocked loudly on the door.

"Pooh Bear!" Christopher Robin exclaimed. "What a wonderful surprise! Come in!"

Pooh was led into Christopher Robin's toasty den, ablaze with lights and colors dancing merrily from candles to glass balls to tinsel and back again!

"My!" Pooh breathed. "This certainly looks like Christmas! So I suppose I can ask you what I came to find out," he rubbed his chin thoughtfully, "as soon as I remember what it is."

But then Pooh frowned and stepped up to Christopher Robin's fireplace, where a row of socks and stockings of all shapes and sizes hung neatly from the mantelpiece.

"Don't you think," Pooh remarked, trying to look as wise as possible, "that Christmas is, perhaps, not the best time for drying your laundry?"

"Silly old bear," Christopher Robin laughed, ruffling the fluff on Pooh's head. "That's not laundry. They're stockings to hold Christmas presents!"

"You mean," Pooh answered slowly, trying to take it all in, "you have to have stockings to put presents in?"

"Yes," said Christopher Robin, "that's the way it's done."

"Oh bother!" said Pooh, looking down at his feet. Not only did he have no presents for his friends, but they had no stockings to put the presents in! Pooh, being a bear, had little use for stockings, bare feet being, after all, one of the things bears are used to. All his friends in the Hundred-Acre Wood were much the same way.

When Pooh mentioned this, Christopher Robin laughed. "Come with me, Pooh Bear. I have plenty of stockings for everyone."

Christopher Robin showed Pooh a drawer containing socks and stockings of every size, shape, and color.

"These are all stockings who have lost their mates and would love to have someone with whom to share Christmas," said Christopher Robin. He scratched one of Pooh's ears. "It's the thought that counts, you know."

"Why, yes," replied Pooh, happy that Christopher Robin had remembered to answer the question that he had forgotten to ask. "Thank you very much, Christopher Robin."

Soon Pooh was walking happily home with his arms full of stockings. The snow had stopped falling, leaving a wonderful white coverlet over the entire forest. It was as if the Hundred-Acre Wood had decorated itself for Christmas. A huge moon made it seem as bright as day.

"But," Pooh reminded himself with a yawn, "it is very late, and I must get these stockings delivered." He considered for a moment. "I must get everyone presents, too, of course, but the stockings come first."

And so Pooh, being as quiet as the soft night around him, crept into his friends' homes one by one and left a stocking, with a little note "From Pooh" hanging from each one's mantel.

First, of course, there was Piglet's house, where Pooh placed a very small stocking.

He then left a striped one for Tigger because he was sure that was the sort of stocking Tiggers like best.

32

Pooh left a very bright orange one at Rabbit's house.

Eeyore got the warmest and friendliest stocking Pooh could find.

Gopher received
a long, dark
stocking. Pooh
thought it was what
a tunnel would look
like if a tunnel
were a stocking.

Finally, Owl was given
a stocking the color of the
sky—in which, Pooh
thought, he would like to
fly if *he* were Owl.

It was very, very late when Pooh nailed his own honey-colored stocking to his very own mantelpiece.

"Now that this stocking business is all taken care of," said Pooh, settling down in his softest armchair, "I simply must do some serious thinking about what I am going to give my friends for Christmas." Pooh closed his eyes, and soon neither his snoring nor the sun rising over the Hundred-Acre Wood disturbed his thoughts.

In fact, Pooh did not stop his deep thinking, or loud
snoring, until a knock sounded at his door, accompanied
by a chorus of "Merry Christmas, Pooh Bear!"
   Pooh opened his eyes and glanced about anxiously.

"Oh no!" he thought. "My friends are here for Christmas and I have no presents for any of them!"

"There's only one thing to do," he told himself sternly. "I shall simply have to tell my friends I'm sorry, but I only *thought* about presents for them."

Pooh opened his door and started to apologize, but before he could say a word, in rushed all his friends—Piglet, Tigger, Rabbit, Gopher, Eeyore, and Owl—all thanking Pooh at once for his thoughtful gifts.

Piglet was wearing a new stocking cap. "My ears are very grateful, Pooh Bear. It was exactly what I wanted."

Tigger told Pooh how much he loved his new "stripedy" sleeping bag. "It's cozier than cozy!"

Rabbit couldn't wait to tell how he'd always dreamed of owning a color-coordinated carrot cover. How could Pooh possibly have known?

Gopher appreciated the "bag" for toting around his rock samples. "Never had one big enough before!"

Eeyore explained—if anyone was interested—that his tail had never been warmer than in its new warmer.

Owl was positive his brand-new "wind sock" would provide him with all the necessary data required to prevent the occasional crash landing through his dining-room window!

Pooh put his hands behind his back and looked thoughtful. "Something awfully nice is going on, though I'm not at all sure how it happened."

"I'll tell ya how it happened, buddy bear," exclaimed Tigger. "It's called Christmas!" He shoved a large pot

of honey, with a "stripedy" ribbon and bow, down the stocking hanging from Pooh's mantel. The others quickly followed suit with presents of their own for Pooh, which all turned out to be pots of honey. What else would a Pooh Bear want for Christmas…or any other time?

"Christmas," sighed Pooh happily. "What a very sweet thought indeed!"